Laila Bailee

The Tooth Fairy Stole my Headphones

Ok, so let's get one thing straight:

I DO NOT TELL STORIES! I'm Laila Baila and I'm 6 years old.

That's right, this is big-kid business.

My parents don't make up things we kids can't trust, and we

kids don't do it to them either. "Tell the truth."

That's the rule in our house. Plus, I'm a big girl

now. I don't get in much trouble.

I get to ride on the school bus like my brother Alex in middle

school, and my sister Kayla in high school.

I'm big enough to get on the dance team at the

Recreation Center if I want, (I already asked).

I like to eat Blow Pops, candy corn, gummy worms, Sweet

Tarts, and a whole bunch of other stuff my teacher,

Mrs. Ruby, gives our class on Friday Fun Days.

If I were the type of kid who made up stories all the time,

and didn't tell the truth, my dad would

not let me eat candy

But I don't just love candy, I love all kinds of things.
I love roller skating, playing with
my dog Ollie, dancing, video games,
and I really love music. Music makes me happy
even when I've had a bad day.
Sometimes I will listen to my jams
or play my video games a little too loud
on the tablet. Because of this, my mom bought me a pair
of brand-new sparkly
headphones with butterflies on them. They look super cool!
The bad news is, I can't find them
anywhere, and I've looked everywhere.
The good news is, I'm a super-smart girl and I think I've
figured out what happened. I'll only
tell if you promise not to laugh,
or say I made it up. That way
we can get to the bottom of this mystery together.
Deal? Okay, deal. Remember, don't laugh:
THE TOOTH FAIRY STOLE MY HEADPHONES!
When I catch her I'm going to sic my dog Ollie on
her big head.

That's right, "Sic, Ollie, sic!" Ollie just stares at me.

Well, Ollie doesn't really know how to sic

anyone. (I would know, my brother tried

to sic him on me).Ollie's just too happy

to bite anyone.

Right now he's the

only one who believes me,

(except for you of course),

so we are a team and I

have a plan. "Muah ha ha ha!!!

I love evil laughing"

Ollie knows how to run around in circles really

fast to make himself dizzy. It makes me dizzy

watching him. I decided to use this trick on the

tooth fairy to catch her. Brilliant, isn't it? Ollie

hears everything at night, so when she visits he's going

to get her super dizzy until she falls over

from watching him and then "BAM!"

I'll jump out and tie her to my bed until my mom is awake

and ready to bust her up! That's the best idea

I have right now for catching the thief, so it will have

to do.

This is how I figured it all out: this morning,

when I was eating a plum at breakfast, one of my

teeth came out. My mom looked really close at the tooth

to see how well I had been taking care

of it when it was still in my mouth.

She said it looked white and clean, but could

be better if I didn't

eat so much sweet stuff on Fridays.

She gave me one dollar and said

if I laid off the candy, and

made sure to brush my teeth at night and in the morning,

she would give me two dollars for the

next tooth. I told my mom that was awesome!

And we shook on the deal.

When I got to the bus stop I saw my neighbor, Avery.
I couldn't wait to show off the hole in my
face. Avery had already lost 3 teeth.
She is in the second grade and thinks she knows
everything. "I finally lost a tooth!" I shouted. Avery stared at me with one
eye brow raised before asking me the craziest question.
"How much do you think
the tooth fairy will give you for it?" "The tooth fairy?"
I asked. Avery explained.I told her I didn't think any tooth fairy
ever came to my house. Avery scrunched up her face and
told me I was silly. "Everyone knows the tooth
fairy collects all the teeth and leaves money,
" she said. Then she told me that when
her tooth came out she put it under her pillow. The
tooth fairy came into her room while she was sleeping, took the tooth,
and left her some money. "Five whole dollars,
" Avery said. "Your mom is probably getting
the money and only gave you a dollar."
"My mom wouldn't do that," I said. "I trust my mom."
Avery is kind of mean. I tried to explain to Avery that her mom
probably let the tooth fairy in but Avery said no, the tooth fairy
magically comes in your house while you sleep.
I said, "Wait a minute. A stranger can come in my
house while I'm sleeping and swap out my stuff
without asking me? That is very creepy!"
Avery said she only takes teeth.
But how would Avery
know? She's never even seen the lady.
Avery doesn't even know how she got in her house.

Magic? Yeah, right. My Black Girl magic doesn't

allow me to just break

into anyone's house and

swap out their stuff.

Mom says our magic is our

power and we should only use our power for

good! Then I remembered.

I've been looking all over

for my sparkly headphones and I can't find

them anywhere.

That has to be it!

"Your tooth fairy stole my headphones!"

I yelled at Avery. But

she didn't believe me and

she burst out laughing

Now I'm thinking about it all day.
My teacher, Mrs. Ruby, tells me
to focus in class. I'm trying but
I can't help myself. I can't
stop thinking of ways to catch
a fairy. What other things did she take
that I thought I had lost? There's my green purse with
the sparkling stars on it that Granny sent
me, the glittery jump rope Kayla taught me how to
jump rope with, and the fluffy red bird with
the shiny yellow feet that Alex gave me for making an "A"
on my spelling test. There is also my
light- bright dancing shoes that glow in the dark and,
can you believe, I blamed the missing shoes
on Ollie? I found a squeaky toy where I thought I'd
left my glow shoe. Now, I know the tooth fairy
took my shoe and left me a dog's chewed up
squeak toy in its place. What kind of deal is that?
Ollie is such a perfect and good dog he would
never do a thing like that. Now I feel bad about
being so mad at him. "You're such a good boy,
Ollie. Oh, yes you are a good dog. Smoochie,
smoochie." Where was I again?
Oh right, the thief!

I found the tooth I had lost wrapped

in a tissue on my mother's dresser.

When it was time to go

to bed, I placed the tooth under my pillow

and settled into bed. Ollie took

his position on the rug

next to my bed. Neither of us made a sound

but no tooth fairy came.

We were on the lookout for

two nights in a row, but still no tooth fairy

. I was getting tired of looking out for her and Ollie

wanted to go sleep in his own bed

next to my brother. By the second night,

Ollie started whining

at my door to get out.

The next morning, while I was eating my
toast and apple slices for
breakfast, another tooth came out! That's it,
I thought. The tooth fairy wasn't coming because I
didn't have any new teeth out! I knew exactly
what to do. I asked my mom if I could keep the
tooth for one night. She looked puzzled but she gave me
a dazzling little silver pouch to keep it
in so I wouldn't lose the tiny prize. As soon as I put it under
my pillow, Ollie jumped up and
snatched the pouch off of my
bed and ran outside into the back
yard! I chased him as fast as I
could. "Wait, Ollie!" I finally caught up to him as he was
digging a hole on the side of the yard.
"Ollie!" I gasped in surprise. I see my sister's glittery jump rope,
the green sparkly purse from
Granny, and my red bird with the shiny feet from Alex.
I couldn't believe it but my brand new
sparkly butterfly head phones
were in the hole covered with dirt.

"Oh Ollie, not you! My own flesh and blood,"

I cried out loudly.

"How could you do this to me?"

I flopped in the grass to die.

"I will never forgive you," I said.

" I am so mad. I need a happy song."

Ollie walked up to me with my

glittery pouch in his mouth.

He dropped it on my belly and licked my ear.

It tickled and I laughed.

He looked so happy

and I knew he was sorry.

I guess Ollie isn't so

perfect after all. He just has to understand

the rules of this family.

Stealing is the same as lying,

right? I'll have to ask Kayla but it all sounds bad.

Maybe he thought he could get doggy magic

from all my shiny stuff. I rubbed his back.

Sorry Ollie, momma says your

magic comes from your

love within. Don't worry, I'll teach you about

magic. Until then, I'm taking all my stuff back!

Hey, did you laugh?

Made in the USA
Monee, IL
18 August 2021